Pippin at the Gym

Pippin
at the Gym

Phylliss Adams
Eleanore Hartson
Mark Taylor

Illustrated by Gwen Connelly

Follett Publishing Company
Chicago, Illinois

Atlanta, Georgia · Dallas, Texas
Sacramento, California · Warrensburg, Missouri
Flemington, New Jersey

3906

LC 82-082454
ISBN 0-695-41681-2
ISBN 0-695-31681-8 (pbk.)

"Look, Herbie," said Pippin.
"People are going to the gym.
I can show them how to jump.
I'll go there, too."

Pippin jumped into the gym.

He jumped over to some people.
Then Pippin sang.

Jump, jump, jump!
It's good for you.
I will show you
What to do.

The people looked at Pippin.
And Pippin sang to them.

> All you women
> And all you men,
> Let us count
> From one to ten.

> One, two,
> Touch your shoe.
> Three, four,
> Touch the floor.

8

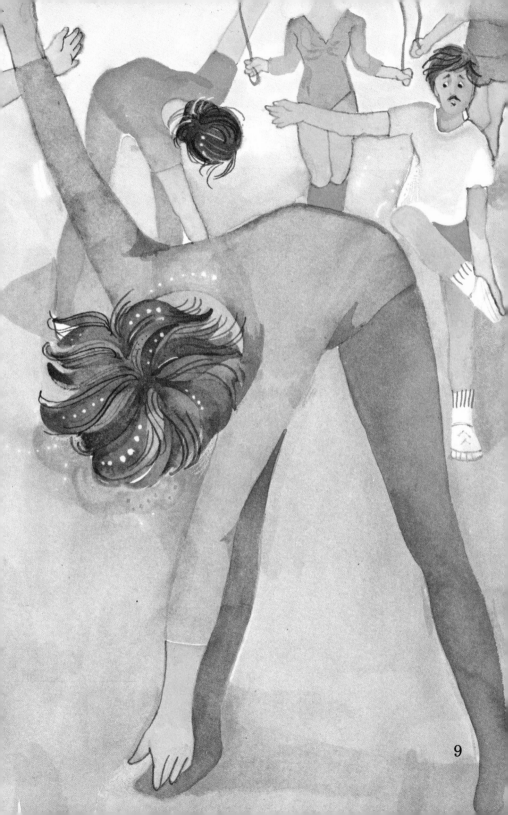

9

Then Pippin looked at some
people jumping rope.
He jumped over to them and sang.

Five, six,
Do your kicks.
Jump and hop.
Do not stop.

Two men were tired.
They stopped to rest.

Then Pippin saw some men and
women working hard.
He jumped over to them and sang.

 Seven, eight,
Lift that weight.
Nine, ten,
Do it again.

Now some more people stopped to rest.

Pippin jumped over to some
men and women.
He sang to them.

Keep on going.
You will be done
When I count
From ten to one.

Pippin saw some people getting
something to drink.
He jumped over to them and sang.

 Ten, nine,
Keep in line.
Now eight,
Don't be late.

17

Pippin went over to some people who were jumping.
Pippin sang.

> Seven, six, five,
> Now look alive.
> And four and three,
> Now bend your knee.
> And two and one,
> Oh, what fun!

The people were tired.
They stopped to rest.

Now only one woman was jumping.
Pippin sang to her.

Jump and hop.
Do not stop.

But then the woman stopped to rest, too.

Pippin sang to all the people.

> Get up!
> Get off the floor.
> Keep on going.
> Do some more.

But the people were too tired to get up.

One man said to Pippin,
"We are very tired, Pippin.
Please go away."

As Pippin jumped out of the gym,
he sang.

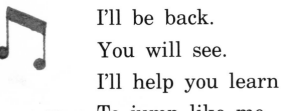

I'll be back.
You will see.
I'll help you learn
To jump like me.

"Here I am," Pippin said to Herbie.
"I had fun in the gym.
I told the people how to jump.
And now I'm a little tired."

Pippin jumped into Herbie's pocket.

Then Herbie looked at Pippin and sang.

Here in my pocket,
See who I keep.

Tired little Pippin,
Sound, sound asleep.

Pippin Says

If necessary, read these directions to the child:
Play a game with Pippin.
Read each sentence.
Then do what Pippin says.

Pippin says, "Hop on one foot three times.
Then hop on the other foot two times."

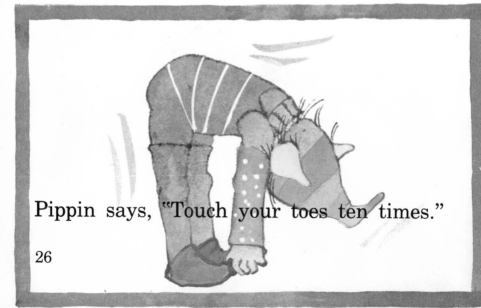

Pippin says, "Touch your toes ten times."

26

Pippin says, "Jump up and down as you count from one to ten."

Pippin says, "Put your hands on your head."

A Funny Gym

Pippin went to another gym.
He saw things that did not belong in the gym.
Can you find them?

Ask someone to help you read the poem.
Then read it without help.

The Little Elfman

I met a little Elfman once,
  Down where the lilies blow.
I asked him why he was so small,
  And why he didn't grow.

He slightly frowned, and with his eye
  He looked me through and through—
"I'm just as big for me," said he,
  "As you are big for you!"

                                    John Kendrick Bangs

30

In addition to many of the words used in **The Troll Family Stories** and **The Cora Cow Tales,** the following words appear in the story *Pippin at the Gym*.

again	gym	men	sang
alive		more	seven
as	hard		shoe
asleep	her	nine	six
	Herbie		sound
back	hop	of	
bend		off	ten
	I'll	only	them
count	I'm	over	tired
	into		told
done	it's	people	touch
don't		Pippin	
drink	keep	pocket	very
	kick		
eight	knee	rest	weight
		rope	when
five	late		who
floor	learn		woman
four	let		women
from	lift		
	line		

About the Authors

Phylliss Adams, Eleanore Hartson, and Mark Taylor have a combined background that includes writing books for children and teachers, teaching at the elementary and university levels, and working in the areas of curriculum development, reading instruction and research, teacher training, parent education, and library and media services.

About the Illustrator

Gwen Connelly was born and raised in the Chicago area. After studying Fiber Art at the Penland School of Art in North Carolina and Fine Art at the University of Montana, she returned to Chicago to work as a designer, illustrator, and fine artist. Her talents are now concentrated on illustrating children's books.

Pippin came to life in the French carriage house that is Ms. Connelly's studio. The illustrator lives with her husband, daughter, and cat in Highland Park, Illinois.

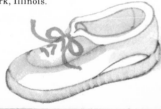

123456789/8786858483